NEW YEAR'S BITE

S.J. TILLY

New Year's Bite

Bite Series Book Three

Copyright © S.J. Tilly LLC 2024

Cover: James Adkinson

Editors: Jeanine Harrell, Indie Edits with Jeanine

& Beth Lawton, VB Edits

This book is dedicated to my readers who love to bake. I love to eat. We're a match made in fiction.

Chapter One

ALICE

....

"His dick looks huge," my cousin Suzy exclaims the second the phone connects.

Sam, sister to Suzy and my other cousin, hums her agreement.

"Hush," I hiss, looking at Michael to see if he can hear them.

But his back is currently to me as he paces through the hotel suite with his phone to his ear, so I'm pretty sure we're safe.

"Oh shit, is Mr. Huge Dick with you?" Suzy barely lowers her volume. "We're not on speaker are we?"

"Suzy." I try to scold her while keeping my volume down.

"What? It's a compliment," she argues.

Sam snickers, and honestly, I don't know why I would've expected anything different from them.

But I'm smart enough to not put them on speaker. And for that same reason, I didn't do a video call. Which is good because I'm sure the redness of my cheeks would give away my thoughts. Because really, I can't hear someone talk about Michael's dick and not blush. Especially since I know they're talking about the hot tub photo.

A photo I've saved to my phone and looked at more than a few times.

I really hope when Michael finds the photographer, he can get the uncensored versions.

"Okay, but for real." Sam finally speaks up. "Are you okay? The photos are obviously super hot, but I'm guessing you guys didn't plant them."

Michael snaps something into his phone as he paces through the open double doors leading from where I am in the bedroom out to the living room part of the suite.

"Yeah, no. We didn't plant them." I keep my voice down. "Michael is furious. Mostly on my behalf, it seems."

My cousins make matching sounds of intrigue.

"I can see why a man like Michael wouldn't want the world seeing his woman with a mouthful of d—"

"Sam!" I can't help my laugh. "You are so crass."

She snorts. "You know I'm right though."

"You are." I sigh. "And it's not exactly a great look for him. Or the show." I bite my lip. "Speaking of which..."

I don't know if it's supposed to be a secret, but considering the show starts airing tomorrow, it's not like it can be a secret for long.

Michael holds his phone in front of him, hanging up his call, then starts a new one.

"What about the show?" Sam asks.

"Well, Pamela got sick and now she can't make it. So." I take a deep breath. "I'm going to judge alongside Michael."

The two of them shriek.

I pull the phone away from my ear and wait for the shrill noise to die down.

"It's bonkers," I say when they're quiet enough to hear me again.

"It's fucking awesome." Suzy sounds like she might be crying.

"It's fucking something," I mumble, still not sure I'll be any good at it.

"I can hear that self-doubt in your tone," Sam chides. "Stop that right now."

I roll my eyes. "Thanks, Mom."

She makes a sound. "I take it the show isn't mad about the pictures?"

"Surprisingly, no. They seem to think it will be good for ratings." I shake my head even though they can't see it. "Seems a little backward to me, but what do I know."

"Drama sells and all that, I guess." Suzy hums.

"Yeah, I guess." I shrug.

"So, is Michael trying to find the photographer, or is he just letting it go?"

I watch Michael pace some more, his free hand clenched at his side.

"I think he said something about hiring a private investigator," I tell them. "But I'm not really sure how all that works."

Suzy whistles. "Me either. But it's cool to have PI money. And if anyone can hunt the fucker down, my bet is on HDM."

I groan. "Do I even want to know what that stands for?"

"Oh, let me guess!" Sam sounds like she's bouncing on her toes.

"Sam," Suzy says like she's calling on her.

"What is Huge Dick Michael."

"Ding, ding! Got it in one!" Suzy cheers.

I do my best not to laugh. "I'm hanging up now."

"Bye! Good luck!" Sam tells me.

"With the dick," Suzy adds.

"And be careful," Sam warns.

"With the dick," Suzy repeats, laughing at her own joke.

"Oh my god, bye." I hang up.

Setting my phone on the bed next to me, I have to admit I feel a little lighter, even if my cousins are ridiculous.

Michael paces back in my direction, and his features soften once his gaze lifts and meets mine.

"As soon as you know, I know," he says to the person on the other end of the line, then hangs up.

I stay put, letting him cross the space to me.

"How are your cousins?" Michael nods to my phone.

"Ridiculous," I answer. "Did you talk to the investigator guy?" Michael nods.

"What did he say?" I cross my legs, making room for Michael.

He lowers himself to sit on the edge of the bed, facing me. "Said he'll start right away."

"Oh wow." My brows lift. "Will he go to the cabin? I don't actually know how this works."

Michael shrugs. "He might end up going, but he sounded confident he could find the identity of the photographer digitally."

"Oh." My shoulders lower.

"Don't sound so disappointed." Michael chuckles. "It will still take detective work. And once he finds the guy who took the pictures, he can find out if anyone put him up to it."

I make a humming sound. "I dunno. That picture of your ass was pretty well framed. It might have been a woman who took them."

Michael gives me a deadpan look, and I only last a second before I crack and laugh.

"Fine." I concede. "You're right, it was probably a man because men are the worst."

Michael dips his chin. "Precisely."

"But what do you mean 'put him up to it'? Weren't we rerouted in the middle of the flight? How would anyone know where to find us?"

"These people can work quickly. And there was an entire plane full of people who knew we were snowed in somewhere near Bear Cove. Even with the last-minute rental, the options were pretty limited, so it wouldn't have been hard for someone to find us."

I scrunch up my nose. "And what, someone went out in the storm searching for a place with the lights on just to take some photos?"

Michael reaches out and takes my hands in his. "Most people aren't like this. I want you to know that."

His tone is so apologetic, and I scoot closer.

I flex my fingers in his. "I know."

He squeezes mine back. "If I thought there was any chance that someone would do... what they did, I'd have kept you inside with all the curtains pulled shut."

I scoot another inch closer until our knees touch. "Underneath the covers, just to be safe?"

His sigh is half humor, half frustration. "I really am sorry, Alice. This isn't the way I wanted to introduce you to fame. My fans are better than this."

"Please don't apologize. You didn't take the photos. You didn't, what, sell them?" I tilt my head, thinking about it. "How much do you think those pictures sold for?"

He shrugs. "Something scandalous like that? Probably ten grand an image. Maybe more. Maybe a lot more."

That amount of money might not seem like much to Michael, but it makes me want to gag.

"Do you have to buy them back?" Our talk from earlier is fresh in my mind. The one where I admitted to having basically no money, and the urge to gag gets stronger. We both know I can't help pay for it if that's what he has to do.

Michael shakes his head as he runs his thumbs over my wrists. "There's no point. The tabloid is the one that bought them, they got the scoop and the initial major spike in views, but the photos are online now. There's no stopping them."

I slide one of my hands free from his grip and press it to my stomach. "You seem very calm about this."

This being the half dozen photos of us, in the middle of various sex acts, plastered all over the internet.

Michael leans forward, stopping when his nose is just inches from mine. "I'm not okay with it. I'm not okay with the comments and bullshit you're going to have to deal with. And

I'm really not okay with all my relatives knowing what my bare ass looks like."

I bite down on a smile. "I didn't think about that."

"I'm trying not to. But I'm glad it was my ass and not yours. Because your naughty bits are just for me." Michael rolls up onto his knees and pushes me onto my back. "And as much as I don't want anyone else to know what your face looks like when you come, I'm glad the world knows you're mine."

I reach for him. "Michael."

With me flat on my back, Michael drops his weight over me. "And I don't like that people know what you look like with a dick in your mouth. But I do like how greedily you swallowed me down."

My legs spread on their own, and Michael's arousal presses against my center.

I roll my hips and whisper his name this time.

He rocks into me. "So, to answer your question, I'm not calm, Sweetness." He rocks his hips again. "I'm not calm at all."

He lowers his face.

His lips a breath away from mine.

And then someone knocks on the door.

My nostrils flare as I try to tamp down my annoyance.

I'm usually good at controlling my emotions. Or at least keeping them off my face. But this rollercoaster of a day has been a fucking struggle.

The drop of depression at having to leave that little cottage when all I wanted to do was stay there, in bed, with my woman,

The spike of rage at finding those photos, on display, in the fucking airport.

The lust at examining the photos.

The satisfied joy at learning Alice will be my co-judge on the show.

And now the feel of Alice's soft body beneath mine, but not being able to take out my frustration by filling her in every way I can think of because—the noise sounds again—someone is knocking on our fucking hotel door.

I roll off Alice with a sexually frustrated groan and stomp across the suite.

"Wait!" Alice calls after me, and I hear her feet slapping against the floor as she chases after me. "You can't answer the door like that!"

She grips my wrist.

"Like what?" I growl, not angry with her, just the situation.

She doesn't flinch at my tone. Instead she snickers. "Like that."

Alice reaches out with her free hand, and I jolt when she cups my dick through my pants.

My cock throbs, reminding me that I'm hard, and it's obvious.

"You're not answering the door alone," I tell her, trying not to lean into her touch.

"And I'm not letting the world see any more of your dick than they already have," she retorts.

I take a slow breath, trying to calm said dick, but it's impossible with the heat of her hand against me.

"Fine." I concede. "You can stand in front of me."

She rolls her eyes but steps ahead of me.

There's a third knock at the door.

"Fucking chill," I snap. "We're coming."

Alice mutters something that sounds like *I wish*, but I purposely ignore her. If I start imagining her coming on my dick, it will never deflate.

Chapter Three

ALICE

I swing the door open, then have to jump back when a rolling clothing rack fills the doorway.

"Sorry, coming through!" a woman hidden by the clothes shouts.

Michael's big hands land on my shoulders, and he pulls me off to the side.

He keeps my body in front of his, and I have to stop myself from grinning.

The rack stops, and a pretty woman in her thirties steps out from behind it.

"Hi," she greets. "I'm G, from wardrobe."

A cool name to go with a cool job. And as much as I want to cheer her on for being a boss beauty, I no longer feel like grinning over Michael's boner. If she sees his bulge, I'm going to strangle her with a pair of expensive trousers.

"Hello." I say it quieter than I mean to. "I'm Alice."

"Oh, I know who you are, babe." G winks.

My cheeks heat.

I've never had another woman call me *babe* before.

"Hey, Chef Mike."

"Hi, G," he replies from behind me.

"You really know how to rile up the press, huh?" G snickers, and I'm back to not liking her.

Thankfully, G doesn't say more, just turns to her rack and starts pulling items off.

She has a man's button-down shirt in black and dark wash jeans slung over her arm when she turns around.

"For you." She holds them out for Michael. "I'll check the fit when you have them on, then I want you in the all-black sneakers."

Michael steps around me to take the clothes, and I keep my gaze focused above his belt, not wanting to draw attention to his lower half in case he's still... aroused.

Clothes tucked under his arm, Michael starts to pull his shirt free from his jeans.

"Nope," I bite out and point across the suite. "You change in the bedroom. With the door closed."

I watch him as he tries not to smile. "Yes, ma'am."

I don't look away until the bedroom door clicks shut behind him.

When I turn back to G, she has the biggest smile on her face. "Damn. I don't know which of you I'm more in love with."

"Um..." Having zero clue how to answer that statement, I move my gaze to the clothes. "Are those really for me to wear?"

G spins back to the rack. "Yep." She pulls a pair of navy wide-leg slacks off a hanger, followed by a silver silky long-sleeved top. "I'm pretty good at eyeballing sizes, and I tried to get a feel for your style by rewatching your episodes."

"Oh." I try not to sound horrified at the idea of someone watching the show specifically to figure out my dress size.

She faces me. "Did you and Chef Mike really meet there? Or did you know each other before?"

"We met on the show."

I'm not sure if there are things we're supposed to say or not say, so I figure short answers are best.

"That's so adorable." G makes a show of sighing. "You two

were so... amazing." She lifts one of her hands and fans herself. "And the chemistry was off the charts."

"Uh, thanks." God, I sound as uncomfortable as I feel.

G glances at her watch. "Shit, sorry, we're running behind. Gonna need you to try these on." She thrusts the clothes at me. "This is the one I think will fit best, but I have it in a size up and down if you don't like the feel."

I take the items of clothing and peek at the tag, surprised to see it's the size I'd usually buy. Also surprised she was able to find such pretty items on such short notice.

From my experience, most department stores don't have good plus-size options, let alone have them in stock.

"Are you wearing a thong?" G asks.

I blink at her. "Yes."

She dips her chin. "Good. Panty lines aren't great for promo."

"Wait, what is this for?" I hold up the clothing. I assumed it was just for us to wear tomorrow.

It's G's turn to blink. "Promo. You'll wear it for the first episode too, but we have a photo shoot in five minutes. So strip."

"Five?" I squeak and forget all about being shy as I drop the clothes onto the couch, and then, standing in the middle of the living room area, I shove my pants down.

She can't see Michael undressed, but I don't really care if she sees me.

I'm bent over, pulling my pants free, when I hear the bedroom door open behind me.

There's a curse.

Then the door shuts again.

G snorts a laugh.

And I hope the day can only get better from here.

Chapter Four

MICHAEL

When Alice stands from the hair and makeup chair, it takes all my will power not to stride directly to her and slam my mouth to hers.

But I don't do that.

Because I have *some* self-control.

Also because her makeup looks perfectly applied, and I won't be responsible for messing it up.

As she nears, the bright lights shine across her features, and I notice how glossy her lips are.

So glossy they're almost obscene.

But maybe that's just me, picturing her in the hot tub, with my cum dripping off her mouth.

I clear my throat as she stops before me. "You look beautiful."

Alice beams. "You look pretty handsome yourself."

"Alright, lovebirds." A new woman, this one with a still camera, snaps her fingers. "Let's get this literal show on the road."

Chapter Five

ALICE

We follow the photographer's directions as she has us stand in various locations and poses on the set.

It's surreal to be back on the *Second Bite* set. Or rather, the traveling version, not the actual set out in California.

When I first walked out between the workstations back in Minnesota, I knew it would be a life-changing experience. I knew I'd never be the same.

And now...

Now I'm back on set.

In Canada.

With Michael.

As a freaking judge!

"Finally." The camerawoman huffs.

Wondering what we're doing wrong, I jerk my gaze over to the photographer, but she's talking to Joey, who's striding across the room toward us.

"Come over here." She points at me and Michael.

Joey continues to saunter, unbothered by her tone.

He's been the host of *Second Bite* for years, so he's probably used to the bossiness of some of the crew.

He's not as popular as Michael, but he's good looking and outgoing, as TV hosts usually are.

"Hey, Alice. How nice to see you again." His smile tells me he's seen the photos, and I feel myself blushing again.

I really need to just accept that every human on Earth has probably seen the photos and deal with it.

"Mike." Joey tips his head at Michael.

Michael grunts in reply.

"Joey." The photographer snaps her fingers. "Stand between these two."

I start to step away from Michael to make room, but a hand clamps down on my shoulder.

"No." Michael's gruff tone leaves no room for argument.

The photographer sighs but doesn't complain, just directs Joey to stand a few inches to my right.

Michael stays plastered to my left side, his arm still draped across my shoulders, and I can totally picture him stretching his hand out, shoving Joey away if he gets too close.

Placing my hand in the middle of Michael's back, I look up at him.

As expected, his face is set in a scowl, and I bite my lip in an attempt to keep my smile under control.

There's a flash.

"Perfect. Hold that."

Me?

I look over at the photographer.

"Alice. Stop moving." She bites the words out.

My mouth pops open, embarrassment flooding my cheeks.

There's another flash.

Joey chuckles at my side, and I turn my head to look at him.

Apparently not liking that, Michael tightens his hold on me, forcing my body to aim toward his even as I look over my shoulder at Joey.

Another fucking flash.

———

The cousins won't stop sending me audio clips of themselves laughing.

For some reason, I thought the promo photos would take longer to be posted. As in, maybe tomorrow morning before the first episode. I was not expecting them to go viral an hour after we finished shooting them.

The pictures are pretty entertaining. And even though I'm the one who looks ridiculous, I can see why they used them.

There are a few of just Michael and me, but the three photos of us with Joey are popping up everywhere.

Me gazing at Michael, every bit of my love for him obvious in my expression.

Me with my mouth and eyes wide open, looking guilty as hell pressed into Michael's side.

And me hugged against Michael's body, looking over my shoulder at Joey, who's smirking at both of us.

I didn't look at the online comments.

I'm not interested in hurting my own feelings.

But my cousins sent me screenshots of the best ones.

Anyone else still just thinking about that hot tub picture?

Fuck me, I hope they have babies immediately.

Would pay so much money to see Chef Mike punch Joey in the face for looking too closely at his girl.

We all pretending we wouldn't prefer an episode of Naked Bite?

Back in pajamas, I drop onto the bed.

After the photo shoot, we came up to our room, and I carefully removed my clothes, making sure to smooth out any wrinkles as I hung them up.

Michael said he had to run out to take care of something, probably tabloid related, so I put on my pajamas and ordered room service.

Tomorrow is the first day of filming, and as much as I want

to be at Michael's side, I don't know anything that would help out in the investigation.

I shimmy under the covers.

I don't want to go to sleep without Michael, so I'll wait up for him. But I can just rest my eyes.

Chapter Six

MICHAEL

Nodding, I sign the slip of paper in front of me. "I need it in two days."

The jeweler's eyes widen. "Two?"

I set the pen down. "Two."

Chapter Seven

ALICE

Something beeps.

Then beeps again.

My eyes pop open.

My brain feels scrambled, trying to remember where we are, as I start to sit up.

But then a heavy arm tugs me back down.

"Snooze it, Baby." Michael's voice is scratchy.

"What?" My own voice comes out wonky.

The beeping continues, and I connect the dots.

Reaching out, I slap my hand around on the nightstand until I find my phone.

It goes silent.

"Sorry, I meant to stay up." I rub my eyes. I'd really only meant to close them for a moment, but the light around the edges of the closed curtains tells me that moment was about seven hours.

"You needed the rest." Michael yawns as he says it, and I smile. "Now close your eyes and hush."

My smile turns into a grin. "So grumpy in the morning."

He grunts in reply.

I pat the arm that's over me. "I'm going to shower. If I fall back asleep, I'll just have stress dreams about being late."

"Fine," Michael groans. "Abandon me."

I lean over and kiss his cheek, then wiggle out of bed.

Today is the first day of the New Year's Special. And like the holiday special I was a contestant on, this one is also live streamed. Which means I need to find the right caffeine level between alert and sprinting to the bathroom.

————

"Places, everyone!"

Oh god, oh god, oh god.

"We're going live in three... two..." The man behind the camera holds up a single finger. The big light in the front of the room flashes red. And my heart stops.

How is this even worse the second time around?

But unlike the first time, I'm at the front of the room, and Michael is flexing his fingers around mine.

I take a breath and feel a little calmer as I squeeze his fingers back.

Michael will be at my side, literally, through every step of the show.

I can do this.

Joey starts his usual introduction to the show, and I finally realize that the four workbenches in front of us are empty.

When we did the holiday show last week, the four of us were at our benches before the cameras went live.

That's weird.

"And we have a few special treats for you today, no pun intended." Joey chuckles at his joke. "First, judging alongside her beau, Chef Mike, we have the lovely Alice Hatter joining us." He sweeps an arm out in my direction.

Reminding myself this is live, I give my best smile. "Thanks, Joey. I'm excited to be on this side of the apron today." Then I remember why I'm here in the first place. "But, uh, wishing Pamela a speedy recovery."

I have a second of panic as I wonder if her illness is supposed to be a secret, but then Joey nods his head.

"I talked to Pamela this morning, and she's confident she'll be sipping champagne by the New Year." Joey moves around to Michael's side, continuing the intro to the show. "And, of course, we have the one and only Chef Mike, who we all know is *healthy* like a horse."

He emphasizes the word healthy, and I have to work to keep my expression even.

Joey can't possibly be alluding to the term *hung like a horse* on live TV.

Could he?

I didn't think to ask anyone about the... pictures. I just assumed no one would make any jokes or comments. That we would all pretend it never happened.

Michael doesn't react. He just does what he always does during the intro. He gives a silent nod to the camera.

Except it's not the same as always because Michael usually has his arms crossed while he mean mugs. But today he can't. Because he's holding my hand.

"And the second surprise today..." Joey drums his hands on his thighs. "To celebrate the New Year right, all our contestants are celebrities!"

Celebrities?

"Oh hell," I think I say.

Then I sway.

Chapter Eight

MICHAEL

Alice's grip loosens on mine, and she starts to lean lazily away from me.

Spinning toward her, I grip her shoulders.

"Alice." I hold her steady. "Look at me. Are you okay?"

She blinks.

"Alice," I say sternly.

"Sorry. Sorry. I'm okay." Alice glances around. "The surprise was surprising." She tries to laugh.

"Dammit, Baby Cakes." I huff out a breath. "You took a damn year off my life. Are you sure you're okay?"

"Totally fine." She leans around me to lift a hand at one of the camera guys. "Just excited for the contestants."

Someone on set chuckles.

Sighing, I slide my hands down her arms, then move back to her side.

"That was fun. Alrighty." Joey grins at us. "Chef Mike and Baby Cakes, you ready to meet your contestants?"

I want to strangle him for daring to call her that. But shouting at him during a live-stream episode will only ensure that everyone will call her that. And it was my fault for saying it. So instead of inflicting bodily harm, I just stare daggers at Joey.

"Um, yes, please." Alice's answer is soft, but our body mics are sensitive, so they pick up every little sound.

Joey turns toward a door at the far side of the spacious room. "It's my pleasure to introduce the four celebrities competing this weekend. First up, we have the Oscar-winning actor, and stealer of hearts, Drake Daniels."

The door opens, and I recognize the man who steps through.

Drake walks up to the first workstation, the one closest to us, and grins. "Pleasure to be here."

I've watched some of his action movies. He's a good actor.

He's also known for being very good looking.

I squeeze Alice's hand. My silent warning for her not to stare at him.

"Next." Joey pauses as the door opens again. "We have Colby Canterbury. Stand-up comedian with a no-longer-secret knack for baking."

Colby stops at the table across from Drake. "Jokes and yokes. I'm here to serve both."

I've heard of this guy but have never seen his act.

I'm annoyed they're springing this celebrity shit on us without warning. I'm not just the talent, this *is my* show. I should know about things like this. Not only so I can be prepared, but so I can vet the guests. Make sure no one is problematic. Make sure they don't choose someone I have an issue with.

I bite back the urge to growl.

So far the contestants are fine, but I'm still gonna have someone's neck later.

"Baker number three is the talented and brilliant Canadian pop singer, Zelle," Joey announces, and Alice gasps.

A short woman with long brown hair moves to the bench behind Drake. "Hello."

"Oh my god, I love her so much," Alice whispers beside me.

I have to fight my smile. The contestants can't hear her, but her sentiment is still being live streamed. I'll have to remind

Alice tonight that every word is picked up and just hope she doesn't say anything sexy to me before the end of the challenge.

"Last but never least." Joey lifts a hand toward the door. "Amber Addison."

My head snaps over to look at Joey.

He says something about Amber being a popular soap opera actress.

Mentions something else.

But I'm not listening. Just watching.

Joey doesn't look any different than usual.

Isn't acting like a guilty man.

Isn't acting like anything is wrong.

So maybe he doesn't know.

But someone knew, and inwardly, I seethe as my ex-girlfriend walks to the fourth and final workbench.

The redhead lifts her hand. "Hi, Joey. It's so good to be here."

Chapter Nine

ALICE

I'm going to hyperventilate.

This is too much.

Drake reaches across the table and shakes my hand.

Drake doesn't do it for me anymore. Michael is the only one with the keys to my gift box now, but everyone in the world finds Drake attractive.

I think I'm supposed to say something, ask something, but all I can do is smile at Drake.

Michael moves his hand to the center of my back, and I let go of Drake's hand.

"What are you making for today's challenge?" Michael asks.

Drake smiles that lopsided smile he's famous for. "Lemon and ginger cake."

As he starts to talk about the ingredients, I let myself remember all the episodes of *Second Bite* that I've watched over and over again.

I know how to do this.

I know how this is supposed to go.

And as we move on, I get into the swing of it.

I ask the questions.

Hum at *hopefully* the right times.

And do my best not to scrunch my nose when Colby tells us he's making a tomato cake.

Michael seems to know what it is and is excited about trying it, but I think it sounds disgusting.

We talk to Zelle, and I have to stop myself from leaning down and resting my chin on her work top because her talking voice is just as pretty as her singing voice, and I could listen to her all day.

Not to mention, she's just as pretty in person. I know the trolls online are always making comments about her weight, but I just think it's awesome to see such a successful artist who's my size.

"Good luck," Michael tells Zelle, then I swear he grumbles as Joey leads us to the final contestant.

I try so hard to keep my smile normal, but seriously, how can I? I'm about to meet Amber Addison!

The queen of soap operas.

The master of the instant cry.

The woman who was basically my babysitter after school for years.

We stop before her, and I'm beaming like a fool.

But Amber doesn't look at me. "Hello, Michael."

My smile dims.

Michael. Only his close friends and family call him that.

"Hello." Michael's tone is sharp and causes me to look up at him.

If someone didn't know him well, maybe they wouldn't catch the difference. But I can hear it. He's tense.

Joey clears his throat, familiar enough with Michael's habits.

Trying to remain unaffected by whatever is happening, I hold my hand out to Amber. "Hi, it's so great to meet you."

Her beautifully crafted eyebrows lift as she turns her head to look at me.

She takes my hand, not saying anything.

"I'm a big fan," I tell her honestly. "I've been watching you on *Dawns of Agony* since I was a kid."

Amber narrows her eyes. "That's nice."

Her tone is icy, and I worry that what I said came off as insulting when I meant it as a compliment.

She drops my hand and turns to Michael. "I'm going to make an orange spice cake. It might be cheating since it's the recipe you taught me, but at least I know you'll like it."

The recipe you taught me.

Is this bitch implying what I think she's implying?

"So, uh, I take it you two know each other?" Joey asks the question that's thudding inside my skull.

Amber lets out something that I would have called a tinkling laugh a moment ago, but to me she sounds like a braying donkey. "I mean, if dating counts as knowing each other."

Dating.

She dated Michael?

How?

How could I not know that?

"When was that?" Joey asks, sounding as stunned by this information as I am.

"Oh, probably back when *this one* was a kid." She waves a hand in my direction.

This. Old. Bitch.

"Isn't that right, Michael?" Amber reaches out like she's going to touch Michael's arm.

And hand to the cookie gods, I swear time slows around me.

I can hear every heartbeat.

I can feel her exhaled breath as she chuckles.

And I summon lightning through the ceiling. It zaps Amber, and she lights up like a cartoon x-ray. Her full skeleton on display. Her heart nothing but a pile of chewed-on chicken bones.

A large palm grips the back of my neck just as I start to lean forward.

Michael tightens his fingers, keeping me from lunging at this hag.

Teeth clenched, I glance up at him.

His mouth is flat, but his eyes are on fire. And I see he's put his other hand in his pants pocket, keeping it out of Amber's reach.

The knowledge settles me. Just a little.

"Welp." Joey claps once. "Good luck with your cake."

Fuck this lady and her cake. I want to shove those oranges up her nose.

Michael uses his hold on my neck to steer me away from the source of my fury.

Away from Amber fucking Addison.

Alice is practically vibrating under my palm, and I hate that she's upset. Hate that this is happening to her on live TV.

But... I kind of love that she's full of jealousy.

Which is understandable, even if there are zero feelings between me and Amber. Because if the assholes in charge dared to bring one of her ex-boyfriends onto my show, I'd bake him into a six-foot calzone.

"Mi—" Alice starts to say my name, and I flex my fingers against her neck as I guide her away from the contestants.

The clock is ticking on the New Year's fruitcake challenge, and there's no stopping it. So for the next hour and a half, we just have to sit up at the front of the large room, in view of the cameras.

But we won't have to talk to Amber again until judging.

Fucking Amber.

What the fuck were the producers thinking?

Our relationship was never public. Hardly even a relationship. But someone had to know. There's no possible way this happened just by chance.

"Michael," Alice hisses under her breath.

"Baby," I whisper back.

Her eyes are narrowed up at me. "Don't you *Baby* me. Did you—"

This time I cut her off by turning her toward me and gripping her chin.

I mouth the word *don't*.

If she asks me if I knew about this, I'm going to lose it.

I get it.

This is fucked.

I can't even really blame her for wanting to ask it.

But I still hate it. Because she knows me better than that.

Instead of going to the two director's chairs set up for us, I let go of Alice's chin and aim her toward one of the free-standing refrigerators.

I swear I can hear her mouth open, probably to hiss something else at me, so I rush the final few steps.

I put her back against the back of the fridge and crowd into her space.

We're making a scene. There's no way the cameras won't follow us. But I just need to remind her about these fucking microphones and hope she's willing to wait until we get upstairs to discuss this.

I point to my chest, where the small mic is attached to my shirt, next to one of my buttons.

She heaves out a breath. "I know." I start to relax. "You're my Mr. Claus and in charge, but this..."

My moment of relaxation ends.

Alice waves a hand back toward the contestants, and I don't know if I want to slap my hand to my face or burst out laughing.

"Alice," I say it as quietly as I can.

"But she's seen the photos of me suck—"

I slam my mouth to hers.

My lips cut off the rest of her words. Words that I just know were going to be *sucking your dick*.

Alice's body instantly softens into mine, all her tension vanishing against my lips.

And I want to deepen the kiss.

Want to lift her and shove her against the fridge.

Want to bury myself inside her and remind her that she's my one and only.

But we're on live TV.

I pull back, and before she can make that little whiny sound that goes straight to my balls, I press my finger to her lips.

Her eyes are narrowed again, but this time it's because she wants more kisses, not because she's angry with me.

I slowly remove my finger, then bring it directly to the mic on my shirt.

She follows the movement.

Then her gaze jumps back up to meet mine.

I nod once. And mouth *every word.*

Her mouth parts in an O as she finally understands.

Then her eyes widen, probably remembering what she said right before I kissed her.

I nod again, and even though the whole situation is a mess, I can't stop my smile.

Alice reaches out and places a palm over my mic and then one over her own.

"You still love me the most, right?" She whispers it so quietly that it's only for my ears.

She's smiling. But it's a soft smile. One with a hint of insecurity.

I grip her wrists and pull her hands off the mics.

"I'll always love you the most."

Chapter Eleven

ALICE

"Wow." I hold my hand over my mouth as I say it.

I'm not even mad that Amber made this. How can I be mad when this is the fourth cake I've tasted, and each has been just as delicious as the last? Even that weird-ass tomato cake.

Michael nods as he takes a bite.

After spending the challenge time sitting beside Michael while the bakers baked, I was able to look past my own tension to see his. And as much as I hate that his ex was somehow put on the show, I don't want my man to have to deal with a woman he doesn't like. And if that means taking the lead on this tasting, so be it.

"Seriously." I keep going because fuck, this c-word can bake. "I don't care where the recipe came from, the cake is moist and light. You managed to keep the orange flavor bright. And even with the cinnamon glaze, it still feels fresh." I pick up one of the mini stars covered in edible glitter. "And these little spiced cookies are the perfect touch for New Year's."

I pop the cookie in my mouth and find Amber Addison gaping at me.

I pull my shoulders back a bit more as pride fills me.

Take that, soap opera writers! I know how to throw down a plot twist when necessary.

"Yes, well." Amber blinks back her composure. "It's always been a *pleasure* to make in the past."

"I bet," I answer cheerily as I pop another star cookie into my mouth.

I know what she's trying to do.

And I want to pour the rest of her glitter into my hand, then blow it into her face for saying the word pleasure like that in front of *my* Michael.

But I'll settle for moaning around my mouthful while I soak in the feeling of Michael setting his hand on my shoulder.

I don't miss the way Amber watches the movement.

And I don't miss the way her eye twitches.

And I certainly don't miss the fact that Michael is keeping his hand where it is, making no move to lift his fork for a second bite.

When the cameras shut off, I don't waste any time.

Alice turns like she's going to go talk to someone, but I grab her hand to stop her.

I use my other hand to point at the producer about to walk past. "I'll be back down to talk to you." My tone tells him it isn't going to be a friendly talk, and I'm sure it's no mystery what I'm pissed about.

He nods, and I turn away.

Alice doesn't argue or ask where we're going when I start to tug her along with me.

She did amazing today.

Better than amazing. She was fucking perfect. A total natural.

But I know it cost her.

Playing nice and complimenting Amber had to cost her.

Just like in Minneapolis, the *Second Bite* set is in a large ballroom inside the same hotel everyone is staying in. Including us.

The elevator bay is blessedly empty as I stride straight over and press the up button.

"Is there anything else we have to do?" Alice asks, just as an elevator opens behind her. "Or are we done?"

I crowd her backward through the open doors. "We're never gonna be done, Little Sweetness."

She clutches at my shirt. "You know that's not what I meant."

"I know." I pause just long enough to hit the button for our floor. "But I need more of your sweet words right now."

I press her against the back wall of the elevator.

"Sweet words?" Her chest heaves against mine.

"Yeah, Baby. That's why you're my Sweetness. My Sweet Girl. It's not just that candy slit between your legs that makes you so sweet. It's the words that come out of your mouth. It's your words that make me feel so fucking good."

Instead of giving me those words, Alice brings her hands up and grips my neck.

Her eyes are bright while she pulls my face down to meet hers.

And I let her.

My mouth fuses with hers, and I finally get to kiss her the way I've wanted to since this morning.

I push my tongue past her lips.

And she sucks it.

Alice sucks my tongue into her mouth as her nails claw against the back of my neck, and I feel the shape of her settle into my heart.

Every day.

Every day, for the rest of my life, I'm going to come home to this woman.

I wrap my arms around her and hoist her into the air.

Alice lets out a sound of surprise, but when I boost her up, her face becomes level with mine, and she deepens the kiss.

A groan rumbles through my chest when Alice tightens her legs around my waist.

I hear the doors slide open behind me, and I turn, Alice still wrapped around me.

There's a startled yelp from someone who isn't us. And a person blurs past us into the elevator as we exit.

This is hardly more illicit than what the world has already seen, so I decide it doesn't matter that they saw us.

I shift my grip on Alice and get the room key out of my pocket, fumbling for a moment to get the door open.

It slams shut behind us.

And the bedroom is too far away.

I aim for the living room, and when my knees bump against the couch, I drop my girl.

She bounces once with a little puff of an exhale.

I kneel before her.

"Pants off." My demand is hardly necessary since I'm already pulling her zipper down and Alice is already lifting her hips.

I tug them off, thong and all.

"Michael." Alice reaches for me.

I evade her grasp and lower my face between her thighs. "Talk to me, Baby Cakes. Give me those sweet words."

"I don't—" Alice cuts off on a gasp as I press my tongue to her entrance and lick.

Chapter Thirteen

ALICE

Michael is devouring me like I'm his dessert and he hasn't eaten four cakes already today.

A finger presses into me, and electricity zips through my belly.

"Oh my Chef," I breathe.

Words. He wants my words.

But I don't know what to say.

"My-my Love." I reach down and grip his hair. "You're so good to me. I love you so much."

I feel foolish the moment I say it. This isn't good dirty talk. But then Michael moans against my pussy. The vibrations rattle against my clit, and I suddenly don't feel so foolish anymore.

"You're even better than all my fantasies put together." I tell him the truth as he laps at me. "I feel so lucky to have you."

Michael shakes his head, his lips rubbing against my pussy as he does it.

I smile through the bliss.

"I'd feel even luckier," I pant, "if you'd put that big dick of yours inside me now."

Michael's tongue pulls away from my core as he sits up on his knees. "See what a sweet mouth you have?" He reaches down and opens the front of his pants. "And if my Baby Cakes wants to be full of my dick, then that's exactly what she'll get."

I spread my legs wider. "Yes, please."

Michael shoves the front of his boxer briefs down and grips his cock. "Keep talking, Sweetness." He notches the tip of his dick against my entrance. "I want to hear those pretty words until you come."

Michael grips my hips and jerks me toward him as he slams his hips forward.

Chapter Fourteen

MICHAEL

Alice cries out, and I have to close my eyes.

Heat surrounds me, and the way Alice's body is clenching around my length is nearly enough to send me over the edge.

"You're so handsome," she chants, "so strong."

I slide my eyes open as I pull my hips back.

The way Alice talks is so fucking innocent, and yet it's lighting me on fire.

I rock forward and bring a hand between us, pressing my thumb to her clit.

Alice jolts at the contact, and her eyes—which had lowered to where we're joined—snap up to meet mine.

"More," I demand as I start to circle my thumb.

"I love your hands." She clutches at the cushion beneath her. "Your fingers are so big."

"These fingers?" I ask, slipping the middle finger of my free hand through her slickness. "Think you can take both?"

With her head propped up against the back of the couch, Alice looks to where my hands are.

I flatten my hand on her stomach so she can see better, but I keep my thumb where it is, working her clit.

"You want me to shove this finger inside you too?" I ask, wiggling my finger at her entrance against the top of my cock.

I've never done this before, but now that I have Alice, I want to try everything.

Alice's lips part, but she just nods.

I pull back so my dick is almost all the way out, then I slide the tip of my finger along the top of my cock until it's against her heat.

Then I slowly push forward, sliding my dick and finger into her heat at the same time.

"Tell me how it feels," I grit out.

"Good. Oh god, it feels so good." Her hips wriggle as she attempts to pull me deeper. "I feel so full, Michael."

I push both in as far as they'll go.

Alice moans.

I pull out.

Push in.

We create a rhythm.

Alice tightens around me as she gets closer.

I keep moving and rubbing her little clit.

"My Chef." She squeezes her eyes shut. "My Michael."

"That's right, my Alice." I feel my orgasm building. "Taking all of me so well. Now come on my cock and prove you're mine,"

I press my finger inside her pussy as I jiggle her clit, and she bursts.

Her body is writhing, and I don't stop. I can't.

I keep rubbing her clit, and I keep thrusting inside her until it's all too much. Then I follow her over the edge.

Michael is waiting for me, sitting on the side of the bed, when I come out of the bathroom.

With no plans to leave the room, I've continued my tradition of pajamas by dinnertime and pulled my hair back.

I know he still wanted to go down and talk to the producers, so I'm not surprised to see him still dressed in his filming clothes, but I am surprised to see a room service cart next to him.

"Come here." He holds a hand out to me.

Not needing to be told twice, I move to him and step between his spread knees.

"Thank you for what you did today." His voice is full of so much compassion it makes my heart squeeze.

"You don't have to thank me." I take his offered hand and press my other palm over his heart.

"I do." He shakes his head and places his hand over mine, pinning it to his chest. "I didn't know Amber would be here." He presses his hand down harder, like he's worried I'll try to pull it away. "I don't know whose idea it was to bring her here, but their career with *Second Bite* is over."

"You don't—"

"I do," he says again. "Even if..." Michael swallows. "Even if I'd never met you, I'd still fire whoever brought her here. This show isn't about drama. It never should have happened. And certainly not with you, the love of my life, at my side."

"I'm mostly mad that I didn't know you two had dated. I thought I knew everything about you."

Michael's chest rises and falls with a deep breath. "It was twenty years ago. A lifetime ago. And I'll tell you whatever you want to know, but I hope you're okay knowing that it wasn't serious. It was casual and brief, and I would've thought her petty jealousy would've worn off by now. But she was dramatic back when I knew her, and she's already proven she's still dramatic now."

"Kind of have to be dramatic to be in soap operas." I pull a face. "I hate that meeting her has ruined *Dawns of Agony* for me. I watched that show after school like every day."

That gets a small smile out of Michael. "That was pretty perfect when you mentioned watching her when you were a kid. I know you weren't trying to needle her about her age, but it was pretty perfect anyway."

"I guess this is what they mean when they say never meet your heroes." I sigh. "Except Zelle is just as cool as I'd hoped she'd be." I bite my lip. "And Drake is really good looking."

Michael narrows his eyes.

"I'm kidding." I lean down and press a kiss to his lips.

"Better be," Michael grumbles.

"So... what did you order?" I eye the cart.

"A couple options for dinner. Whatever you don't eat, I'll have when I get back."

"I can wait for you."

Michael shakes his head. "After the producers, I need to call my manager. He should have at least known about the celebrity bit. The fact that I was completely in the dark, on my own show, is unacceptable."

I bite my lip.

"What?" Michael watches me.

"You're so hot when you're angry."

He shakes his head. "Go eat your food. I have to run out and grab a few things after my talks, so I'll be a bit."

After a hug and another quick kiss, Michael leaves the room.

Once he's gone, I select the burger from the options and pull out Michael's laptop. While I eat, I can watch the episode of *Dawns of Agony* when Amber's character dies in a freak collapsing-bookshelf accident.

Chapter Sixteen

ALICE

"Let's go to bed, Baby."

I blink into the dark room. "Bed?"

"Yeah, you fell asleep on the couch." Michael starts to tuck his hands under me like he's going to carry me, and I start to sit up. "Just wrap your arms around me."

Too tired to argue, I do as he says. And when he pulls me up off the couch, I wrap my legs around him.

It's just like earlier, him carrying me like this. Except this time, we're going to make it all the way to the bedroom.

I press my mouth to his shoulder to stifle my yawn.

"My sleepy little elf." Michael squeezes me tighter.

"You were gone a long time."

He slides one of his hands up and down my spine. "I know. I'm sorry."

I inhale him. "Why do you smell like vanilla?"

"I'm a baker, remember?"

I hum, my brain already drifting back to sleep, not thinking twice about his answer.

Chapter Seventeen

MICHAEL

"Hello and welcome to *Second Bite*," Joey says to the cameras. "We're on day two of our Celebrity New Year's Special. If you tuned in yesterday, you got to meet our contestants—Drake Daniels, Colby Canterbury, Zelle, and Amber Addison."

I can't even hear her name without feeling anger well inside me.

The producers all played dumb last night. Claiming they didn't know of the history between us, that casting had approved her application and they didn't think twice about it.

I mostly believe them. Though I'll keep digging.

At least my private investigator is competent.

He tracked down where the photo email originated from, and I can't say I'm surprised the location was Bear Cove, the town where the images were taken. So he's heading there today, and by tomorrow evening, I should know if it was someone working on their own, or if they were put up to the task.

"For today's challenge, you all must make a New Year's inspired ice cream dessert. Your dish must have—"

The static in my brain drowns out whatever Joey says next.

It's not supposed to be ice cream.

It's supposed to be cheesecake.

We did ice cream in the last special.

My eyes move to the back corner workstation.

To Amber.

She's looking right back at me, and the smile on her face might look casual to someone else, but I know her moods. She's up to something. And I have a feeling I know what that something is.

I just need Alice to hold her composure because I'm not sure I'll be able to.

Zelle, the beautiful singer, bites her lips and nods. "Yep, a giant ice cream sandwich."

I grin at the idea and look over the ingredients on her workstation. "What flavors are you doing?"

"I really love the classic Neapolitan combination, so I'm sandwiching two vanilla sugar cookies with sprinkles"—she holds her hands out to demonstrate cookies the size of dinner plates—"around a strawberry ice cream, with finely diced fresh berries mixed in, along with dark chocolate shavings rather than the chips." Zelle lifts a shoulder. "I just think the shaved bits melt in your mouth better."

I press my lips together.

I press them together hard.

But it doesn't stop the snort.

Zelle blinks at me, then her blue eyes widen. "Oh god. I meant the chocolate."

I snort again and slap my hand over my mouth.

Michael shifts beside me, lifting his hand to the back of my neck. "It sounds lovely, Zelle. How thick do you expect it to be?"

I croak a laugh into my palm because, seriously?

"Pretty thick," Zelle squeaks as her cheeks turn red.

I feel like I might choke on the laughter I'm trying to hold back.

"Well, good luck." Joey cuts in, moving the show along like the professional he is.

Michael keeps his hand where it is, up under my hair, and I focus on the skin-on-skin contact as I catch my breath and prepare to face off with Amber the Asshole once again.

Joey gets to her bench first, greeting her with his usual happiness.

Amber replies, then turns to look at Michael, and only Michael, once again completely ignoring me.

"What are you doing?" Michael asks her flatly.

And I have to press my lips together again, only this time it's because he sounds so mad, and I can't help but find it arousing.

Amber blinks for a moment, like she was expecting him to be all friendly or something equally dumb, then her face morphs into a wide smile. "I'm making a chai ice cream."

Chai. Ice cream.

A red warning light flashes inside my brain.

She wouldn't...

"What else?" Michael's tone hasn't changed, and I realize he put it together long before we even got to the table.

And my new suspicion is confirmed when Amber replies. "A cinnamon filling."

Red starts to haze around my vision as indignation fills my chest.

Joey clears his throat. "And how are you presenting these items to make them New Year's themed?"

Still ignoring me, Amber turns to Joey. "Well, up here in Canada, New Year's is still winter, so I thought I'd put it all together into a snowman. Really celebrate the season."

"Okay..." Joey takes a step toward Michael, placing a hand on his upper arm like he's getting ready to hold him back. "Good luck."

Before Amber can say anything else, Joey starts to push Michael away from Amber's workbench.

Michael steps into me, and it takes everything I have not to hold up my middle finger before I turn and walk away.

Chapter Nineteen

MICHAEL

"Very original presentation," I tell Drake as I cut a slice of the mocha-baked Alaska he made.

"Thank you." The man, who always looks so self-assured, looks a little nervous.

It never ceases to amaze me how insecure famous people can be when they have to do something outside their usual talent.

"Remind me of the layers," Alice asks him as I set half the slice onto her plate.

"There's a chocolate brownie base with a dome of coffee ice cream. And I added a touch of coconut into the meringue. I've found it gives it more of a marshmallow flavor."

Alice scoops up a bite and puts it in her mouth. "Holy Fu—" I nudge her with my elbow. "Fudgesicles."

Drake beams at her reaction, and as much as I don't want him smiling at my girl, I want her feeling as good as possible as we lead up to Amber.

I agree with Alice about the perfect balance of flavors and get the same giant smile in return.

We move through Colby's dessert. A grasshopper-mint ice cream cake carved into the approximate shape of a champagne bottle, which is tasty even if the design is a bit rustic.

Zelle's giant ice cream sandwich, covered in silver and gold sprinkles, is just as delicious as I'd hoped. The strawberry and chocolate complement the sweetness of the sugar cookie.

And I'm glad the first three were amazing. Because I can't have Amber winning this competition. She proved herself a competent baker yesterday, and I still can't accept a world where Alice doesn't win on my show and Amber does.

But luckily for me, Amber has let her pettiness get the better of her, and it's going to be her downfall. Because one of the things we look at as judges is originality.

And there's nothing original about the cake she made yesterday, especially since she made a point to announce that it was one of my recipes.

And there's certainly nothing original about the dessert in front of her now.

I was thinking she would form her ice cream into spheres and build them into an actual snowman shape.

Figured she'd do something at least a little creative.

But the bitch has literally recreated Alice's ice cream snowman head. Down to the fondant carrot nose and black gingerbread hat.

The difference is the scarf. Instead of Alice's failed Jell-O scarf, which ultimately ruined her ice cream and chance of winning, Amber has created a scarf from red fondant and twisted it around the base of the snowman head.

I want to smash it with my fists.

Want to take a blow torch to it and melt it into a puddle.

The absolute fucking nerve of this woman.

How dare—

"Oh my god, it's perfect!" Alice exclaims.

Her voice is so cheerful it startles me out of my angry daze.

Alice starts to move at my side, and I keep my grip on the back of her neck but let her bend forward.

Amber's eyes lock on my arm, focusing on the fact that I'm touching Alice. That I'm not letting go.

But same as yesterday's judging, Amber doesn't seem to know how to handle Alice's compliments.

"This is seriously impressive." Alice inspects the snowman face a bit more, then straightens. "Exactly what I was going for when I made it last week."

Amber's smile falters.

And I have to resist my own.

I don't know why Amber is acting like the hurt party here. She wasn't even subtle about copying Alice. She did the exact same dessert that was aired just a handful of days ago. And she did it to shove it into Alice's face.

With my free hand, I slide the knife over to Alice. "Do the honors, Baby."

I probably shouldn't be using pet names during taping, but... I don't care.

Alice carves off two slices of the snowman head, and we try it at the same time.

I smile around the spoon.

It's delicious.

And it's Alice's recipe.

Alice moans too.

"Good?" Amber asks, her eyes on me.

"It is." I nod and set my spoon down. "But I hope you have plans to make something original tomorrow since your first two recipes have been remakes, and originality is one of the aspects we judge on."

Amber's smug look fades away.

I don't really want to give her a warning that she's fucked up. I'd love to shatter her little dreams of winning all at once. But when she doesn't win tomorrow, I need the audience to understand why. I can't have anyone questioning my decision, saying it was based off personal feelings. And after what I just said, the audience should be well aware that it's going to be a major long shot for her to win.

Alice grabs the knife again, and I worry for half a heartbeat that she's going to slash at Amber with it, but instead she slices off another chunk of the snowman's face.

"Sorry, gotta snag a bit more." She shrugs. "I really don't see myself making this ever again, even if it is delicious." Alice looks up at me. "I'll share if you'd like."

My admiration for this woman grows every second of every day.

"I'd like that." I slide my hand across to her shoulder and hold her against my side. "Let's take an extra plate from everyone and call it lunch."

"Ice cream lunch is something I can get down with." Joey rubs his hands together. "Welp, that's it for today, folks. Tune in tomorrow for the final challenge and to find out who will win the illustrious title of *Second Bite* champion."

Chapter Twenty

ALICE

I tap my spoon against my lips as I savor the last bit of chai ice cream.

"I can see an idea brewing in your brain." Michael sets his plate on the coffee table in front of us. "What is it?"

"Well, Amber using our recipes has me thinking..." Michael tenses, and I shake my head, setting my plate down and turning on the couch to face him. "No, it's nothing bad. I was just thinking about the scholarship foundation idea. What if we did cooking classes as a way to raise money?"

His brows lift at my idea. "Cooking classes?"

I lift a shoulder. "It might be a dumb idea. We'd either have to do a ton of them or charge a ton of money, but if people like recreating our food..." I shrug again. "It's just an idea."

Michael is nodding. "It's a good idea. And people would definitely pay for it." He rubs his chin. "We could have it be ten grand a head. Have eight stations set up, with two people per station so couples or friends could sign up together."

My mouth drops open. "Ten thousand dollars a person?"

He just dips his chin, acknowledging my question while blowing past it. Like ten freaking thousand dollars for a cooking class isn't the most absurd thing that's ever been suggested.

"We can pick different metro areas to offer them in, but if we do... eight... minus the cost of renting out the spaces and set up... We should be able to raise about a million dollars."

I blink at his math, then whisper, "A million dollars?"

Michael finally takes notice of my shock. "I know it sounds like a lot, but school is expensive. And if you figure around forty thousand as an average, that's only twenty-five kids getting a full ride. Or we can spread it out and do, I dunno, ten-grand scholarships to help with tuition instead of covering it. Then we can help a hundred kids."

He's tipping his head back and forth, doing the math, but my brain can't even keep up. Because all I can focus on is the love I have for this man.

"We could also—"

I don't hear whatever he's about to say because I launch myself across the couch at him.

I circle my arms around Michael's neck and hug him as tightly as I can. "I love you so much."

His chest rumbles against mine as he chuckles. "I love you too, Sweetness."

I keep my steps light as I walk out of the bedroom and across the suite.

I feel bad sneaking out like this, but I couldn't think of a good excuse to leave earlier, and I have so much to do still.

Alice should sleep through the night though. She always does after a couple orgasms.

And it's not that I'm worried Alice would think I'm having an affair if she wakes up and finds me gone. Even with my ex-girlfriend in the building, Alice knows I have zero good feelings toward Amber. What had been indifference before has turned into true disdain after her behavior these last few days.

I just don't want Alice to wake up alone.

Ever.

So I'll need to work fast.

After quietly shutting the door behind me, I make my way downstairs to the hotel kitchen.

Not running into anyone, I use my key and unlock the door.

Then I turn on the lights and get to work.

Chapter Twenty-Two

ALICE

I burrow deeper into the scent of brown sugar and make a humming sound.

Heat wraps around me, an echoing sound of comfort coming from the body in front of mine.

"Morning." Michael's voice is gruff.

"Morning," I mumble against his chest before sniffing his shirt. "You smell like breakfast."

A hand slides down my back to palm my ass. "I bet you taste like breakfast."

I arch my back, pressing my ass into his hand.

Michael slaps it.

I let out a yelp, but my core pulses in response.

"Mr. Kesso," I chastise.

Michael groans and rolls over me.

My legs spread as I settle onto my back, making room for Michael and his length between my thighs.

"Call me that again." He rocks his hips, rubbing his cock against my core. My thin sleep shorts and his boxer briefs are the only barrier between us.

I grab his sides, holding him to me. "Are we going to practice for our cooking class, Mr. Kesso?"

A big hand reaches down and pinches my nipple through my tank top. "If the class gets to watch us do this, then we need to charge more."

A moan gets caught with a laugh in my throat. "Anything for the students, sir."

Michael groans and reaches lower.

I expect him to slide his hand inside the top band of my shorts, but he reaches lower.

My shorts are loose enough that he's able to pull the fabric between my legs over to one side, exposing the fact that I'm not wearing panties.

"Tsk, tsk, Ms. Hatter." The back of his fingers drag across my damp entrance. "Violating dress code on your first day of class."

Holy fucking snowflakes. Michael dirty talking is the hottest thing in the whole wide world.

My chest heaves. "Wh-What are you going to do to me, Mr. Kesso?"

"Punish you." He shifts, moving his hand away from my body. Then the hot tip of his dick slaps down against my slit. "With a pounding."

Michael shifts his hips, then slams into me.

And at the same time, my alarm starts to blare.

It's sensory overload.

My pussy is stretched around him.

My heart is galloping like a herd of reindeer in my chest.

And I can't even hold onto him because my muscles are too weak with pleasure.

"Best come for me quick, Ms. Hatter." Michael's breaths are ragged. "This is the third time your alarm has gone off. You're going to be late for class if you don't hurry up."

"Third time?" I pant.

Michael's hips are moving fast, pounding into me like he promised, and my pulse can't keep up.

Then I really register what he said, and I turn my head to look at the clock.

"Michael!"

He slams into me. "That's not what you call me, Ms. Hatter. Now rub your clit and tell me you're sorry."

Lust crashes over me, and I wedge a hand between us to do as I'm told.

"I'm sorry, Mr. Kesso." My bud is so sensitive that the moment my fingers connect, I feel myself climbing toward the crescendo. "I'm so sorry I misbehaved. Please don't make me late."

"That's a good girl." Michael's body tenses. He's just as close as I am. "Now make yourself come on my cock, Ms. Hatter, and I'll give you that A you want."

That shouldn't be hot.

Just like calling him Santa shouldn't have been hot.

But it is.

And I can't hold back anymore.

Chapter Twenty-Three

MICHAEL

I collapse on top of my girl.

My woman.

And even though I'm sure I'm crushing her, she makes a contented sound.

Then the beeping of the alarm breaks through the blood rushing through my ears.

Right. The show.

Alice must recognize the sound at the same time I do because she starts to push at my shoulders. "Michael, we need to shower."

Still buried inside her, I give my hips a shallow thrust. "I'd need a few minutes, but we could definitely do this again in the shower."

She moans, "Michael."

I sigh and reluctantly pull out of her sweet heat and flop onto my back. "Fine, you can go first."

She pats my arm as she shimmies out of bed. "You're the best."

She tries to keep her thighs pressed together but mumbles something about a mess as she shuffles into the bathroom.

As I work to catch my breath, I stare up at the ceiling.

A lot of things are going to change today.
My whole life is going to change today.
And I've never felt more sure of myself.
I fill my lungs, Alice's scent still clinging in the air.
And I smile.

Chapter Twenty-Four

ALICE

The final challenge starts.

Each baker immediately goes to work on their celebration of New Year's desserts.

Michael and I walk hand in hand to each workstation.

We listen to their ideas. Each baker doing something different.

One hour ticks away.

Then the second.

And I soak it all in.

This will be my last day of judging.

I don't know if they'd even want me to continue on, but I already told the producers I wouldn't. I won't take Pamela's job. I couldn't do that to her or her fans.

Maybe when she decides to leave. *Maybe*. But I think I'll do better behind the scenes.

Joey calls out that there are thirty minutes left.

Michael and I sit in our chairs at the front of the room, and I do my best to remember the stupid microphone.

I do my best to keep my hands off him.

I do my best to ignore the ache between my legs.

Ten minutes left.
Five.
Two.
And it's done.

Chapter Twenty-Five

MICHAEL

We move away from Drake's station and over to Colby's.

"Remind us what you made." Alice takes the lead.

The comedian nods to the spherical cake before him. "This is a lemon and lime marble cake that I've covered in orange buttercream and glitter sugar candies to replicate the ball drop in Times Square."

It's gaudy, and I'm not convinced the candies are edible, but it certainly fits the theme. He even has a stick jutting out of the top, replicating the pole the ball slides down.

"It's fantastic." Alice clasps her hands in front of her, getting closer to the cake.

"Thank you." Colby beams. "But before you cut it..." He reaches under the counter and comes out with a lighter.

He ignites the flame, and that's when I realize what the stick in the middle of the cake is.

It's a fucking sparkler.

"I don't think—" Before I can finish, he's touched the flame to the sparkler.

Alice lets out a laugh of enjoyment when the sparks start flying. But then one of the sparks shoots straight down to the questionable candies covering the cake.

And the whole thing lights up into a miniature fireball.

I grip Alice's elbow and yank her away from the danger, but a candy flies off and lands on the loose sleeve of her bright white top.

The ember blooms as the fabric catches fire.

My heart seizes inside my ribs even as I move to react.

Lunging into her, I engulf her forearm with my hands, hugging it to my body, smothering the fire.

The sparkler is still going, sizzling down to the final inch, but the cake isn't in danger of catching fire again since the entire thing is scorched black.

Colby is standing several feet back from his bench, hands up in front of him in a protective manner.

I look beyond Colby to see Zelle with her hands against her cheeks and Amber fighting off a laugh.

Drake steps up beside us.

"You guys okay?" the movie star asks. "I've been burned a few times on set, so I know some tricks if either of you are hurt."

I loosen my grip on Alice's arm, slowly pulling away to reveal the hole burned into her sleeve.

"Are you hurt?" I struggle to get the words out, fear at seeing my woman lit up in flames still choking me.

"No." Alice reaches across to pluck at her sleeve. "Are you? Did my shirt burn you?"

I want to believe her, but...

I grip her sleeve on either side of the small burn hole and tear the fabric.

It gives way easily, the thin material splitting from her wrist to her shoulder.

"Michael!"

"I need to see." I say the only thing I can.

But when I run my eyes and hands over her arm, I don't find a single mark.

"Michael," she says again.

I drag my hands over her forearm again.

"Mr. Kesso," she sternly hisses.

And my eyes snap up to hers.

Her mouth pulls into a sneaky smile. "Show me your palms."

Calmer, I release her arm and hold my hands out, palms up.

She drags her fingertips over the sensitive skin but doesn't find any burn marks on me either.

The flaming candy must've fallen away as I pulled her against me.

"I'm sorry." Colby finally speaks up. "That wasn't supposed to happen."

Drake snorts a *no shit* before he turns and walks back to his station.

The sparkler finally putters out, and we all stare at the cake.

"We could, um, taste the inside," Alice says beside me.

A tendril of smoke comes up from the center of the cake.

"Or maybe not," she adds.

Colby grimaces. "So... what are the odds I could still win?"

Too pissed about him endangering Alice to joke, I turn away from Colby without another word and guide Alice to Zelle's station.

The girls spend a moment checking in on each other, and I let my heartbeat return to normal.

When they're certain they're both okay, I cut into the stunning fruit tart Zelle has made.

The shortcrust is perfect, the thin layer of peaches on top of the vanilla custard is delicious, and the glazed raspberries and pomegranate seeds are laid into the shape of an exploding firework across the surface.

It's perfectly crafted.

Everything Zelle has made has been delicious. And as long as Amber doesn't create something absolutely outstanding, I can select Zelle as the winner with a clear conscience.

Chapter Twenty-Six

ALICE

The salted caramel cheesecake that Amber made looks appealing, even if it does look like she's flooded the entire top with caramel.

She's used careful piping to write Happy New Year across the surface, but that's it.

It's simple. A little basic. But could still be delicious.

Michael slices into the dessert, and as he's pulling the slice away—the caramel dripping off the edges—I see him smirk.

It's just for a split second. The briefest of moments. But I saw it.

Michael is happy.

And then I see why.

The cheesecake is curdled.

Lumps mar what should be a silky smooth texture.

I take a bite, and it doesn't even matter that her salted caramel is way too salty. She won't win.

I don't like wishing ill will on people.

I want to be someone who supports everyone.

But there's an exception to every rule. And today, Amber is that exception.

Michael sets his fork down. "The caramel is too salty. The

cheesecake mixture has curdled. And you needed to have blind baked that crust because it's soggy."

His words are harsh. Unforgiving. But that's how he always is to people who mess up, so it's not like he's being mean just because it's Amber. And it's not even really being mean if it's all true.

I set my fork down and smile at the soap opera star. "We all make mistakes sometimes."

Mine was the Jell-O scarf.

Hers was this cheesecake.

And Michael's was dating her.

Chapter Twenty-Seven

MICHAEL

I shake Zelle's hand, congratulating her on her win.

And I let Alice see my raised brow when she moves in to give Zelle a big hug.

The cameras crowd in around us, and when Alice steps back, Colby and Drake move in to give Zelle hugs too.

I don't bother looking for Amber. It's no surprise that she's a sore loser. And now that the special is done, I don't have to pay her a single bit of attention for the rest of my life.

Alice stands beside me as Zelle brushes a tear off her cheek. "Sorry." She chuckles. "It feels so silly to cry, but this is the first non-singing competition I've ever won."

Joey grins. "Well, there's no more hiding the fact that you're an amazing baker. And if you ever get sick of singing, you could open a bakery."

Zelle shakes her head. "I know how early bakers have to get up. I'm not cut out for that."

Alice leans her head against my shoulder, and I entwine my fingers with hers.

She looks up at me, a gentle smile on her face. "I can't believe I got to be a judge on *Second Bite*."

"You're a natural at it," I tell her honestly.

Alice sighs. "Hopefully it came off that way because I'm pretty sure I was hyperventilating half the time."

I shake my head, even as my own nerves start to grow. "You were perfect." Then, seeing that Joey is done talking, I heave out a breath. "But we're not quite done yet."

Alice furrows her brows. "What do you mean?"

Joey moves to stand before me. "Ready for the next part?"

I nod, and, with my free hand, I pull my phone out of my pocket.

"What's going on?" Alice looks back and forth between me and Joey, who has turned on one of the large TV monitors on the wall.

I squeeze Alice's fingers. "Just taking care of some business." Then I hit the selection to make a video call on my phone.

As it rings, the TV monitor lights up with my image on one side and a blank image on the other.

Then my private investigator answers, and his face populates the other half.

"Afternoon, Mr. Kesso." His bushy mustache moves with each syllable.

"Hello, Mr. Forde. Are you in position?" I ask.

Nearly everyone on set is gaping at me, Alice included.

I didn't leave her out of my plans for any other reason than I didn't want to cause her any extra stress.

Once I was able to confirm that Joey had nothing to do with any of the schemes against me, I pulled him into my plans, and he happily agreed to help.

"I'm in sight and ready," my PI replies.

My smile is wicked. "Move ahead." Then I glance down at Alice, knowing the cameras and mics will pick up what I say to her. "Mr. Forde is the private investigator I hired. And he's been very productive."

"Oh," Alice says before her brows jump up. "Oh!"

I dip my chin back toward the screen.

Mr. Forde has turned the phone around so it shows where he's going.

And he's going to a middle-aged man sitting alone at a table inside a coffee shop.

The man has his laptop open in front of him and a plate covered in crumbs next to him.

Mr. Forde pulls out the only other chair at the small round table, and as he sits down, he presses the lid of the laptop shut.

The man jerks his hands out of the way. "What the—" Then he notices the phone. And my face staring back at him. "Michael?"

"You've been a hard man to reach," I tell my manager.

"What is this?" He tries to keep his tone even, but I can hear the panic.

"This is part of the show. Since you've decided to involve yourself so much over the past few days, I didn't think you'd mind the screen time."

"Screen time?"

I give a serious nod. "We're still live. And to all our viewers, I'd like to introduce you to my manager. The man who purposefully didn't tell me about the celebrity switch. The man who told casting to put Amber Addison on the show. The same man who talked to the producers two nights ago to tell them I wanted the middle challenge changed to ice cream." I hear a few gasps from the crew around me.

"That was for ratings. It's not personal." My manager tries to justify. "And it's not like it cost you anything to have a little bit of drama."

I grit my teeth. "Your actions caused my woman emotional stress. And that alone is enough for me to end your career."

"End my career?" He raises his voice, then looks around the coffee shop and lowers it. "After all these years, you're going to fire me over this?"

"I'm not going to fire you over Amber and ice cream." His shoulders relax. "But I am going to fire you over the photos."

The world watches as my manager's face pales.

He thought he got away with that.

He thought I only knew about the show shit.

Maybe even tried to distract me with all this Amber bullshit.

But he'd be wrong.

I look down at Alice, whose eyes are wide. "This is the man responsible for our photos being plastered all over the tabloids."

"Your manager? Why?" she asks quietly.

"That's a good question. And it's one I asked Mr. Forde." I look back at the screen. "Seems my lovely manager has had a bit of a spending problem. Too many lavish vacations and fender benders in expensive vehicles. And according to an email recovered from Mr. Forde—to the photographer—my manager had a suspicion I was considering firing him." I sigh. "Which I'll admit is true."

Alice lets out a little snort at my insincere tone.

"I didn't—"

I cut my soon-to-be ex-manager off. "You did. And you did it over email." I shake my head. "Mr. Forde could've dug the emails out, but he didn't even have to. The man you hired to take the photos handed them over, along with his portion of the money you made selling the images." I squeeze Alice's hand. "And we're using that money as the first donation to the *Second Bite* Scholarship Fund. And while Alice and I enjoy our New Year's, you better get back on that laptop and file for unemployment because you're fired."

A hand moves into the frame from behind the camera and drops a cloth bag onto the table.

The sound is loud through the microphone.

"What's this?" My ex-manager glares at the bag.

"Your severance," I tell him. "It's a bag of coal."

Then I hang up.

Chapter Twenty-Eight

ALICE

I feel oddly turned on as Michael slides his phone back into his pocket.

I think we need to revisit the instructor role-playing again tonight.

"Joey, I'm ready for the next part," Michael calls out.

My attention turns to Joey as he opens a pair of doors I hadn't noticed before.

Through it, two people wheel in a table holding a three-tier square cake that looks to be entirely covered in gold leaf.

"What's the next part?" I whisper.

"The next part," Michael whispers back as he pulls on my hand to bring me closer to the cake, "is the rest of our lives."

Emotions tie a ribbon around my throat, making it hard to swallow.

And as we get closer, I notice the words etched into the gold.

The love of my life.

My forever.

Baby Cakes.

Little Alice.

Mrs. Claus.

Mistletoe Eyes.

My Sweetness.

Then I hear it.

The chimes.

My eyes slowly lift, and I watch Joey carefully set something on the top of the cake.

A shiny round gold centerpiece, with candles around the bottom and angels twirling above the flames.

It's the same.

It is the exact same centerpiece that my grandmother would put out for Christmas.

The same thing that I drew for Michael days ago when we were snowed in at that cabin.

It's exactly the same... except for the flash of color, the red and green sparkling in the candlelight on each turn.

Michael lets go of my hand and reaches up to stop the angels from spinning.

And from the top of an angel's head, he picks up a ring.

My hands press over my heart.

And my vision swirls as tears fill my eyes.

Michael gives me the softest smile as he lowers to one knee before me. "Alice." He holds up the ring. The massive princess-cut diamond is set in a band of alternating rubies and emeralds. "I know I've only just met you. And I know this is fast. But I don't need years to know that you're mine. I felt it the moment I laid eyes on you. I can feel the truth of it right here." He places a palm over his heart. "It's the same place I can feel your love for me. It's burrowed there. Made itself a home inside me. You give me warmth. Purpose. And I need the entire world to know it will only ever be you." He lifts his hand from his chest and holds it out to me. "So tell me, Baby Cakes, will you marry me?"

"Of course." I'm nodding and sniffing. "I will."

Michael holds my hand steady with one of his.

He slides the ring onto my finger. "Good. Because we're going to do it on New Year's Eve."

My eyes widen, and a laugh bubbles out of me as I throw my arms around my Chef.

EPILOGUE 1 - ALICE

My cousins both wipe tears from their eyes, and I use a tissue to dab at my own.

When I asked them, Suzy and Sam immediately agreed to walk me down the aisle, which we're about to do.

But it was their decision to wear matching black tuxes.

"You look like you belong in a fairytale." Sam sniffles.

I look down at my red satin dress.

The long sleeves are loose but collared at my wrists, and the neckline plunges almost indecently low. And at my side is a bow, where the sides of the dress tie together.

As my cousins each take a side and we start to walk forward, the skirt splits around my leg, exposing my thigh.

And when Michael comes into view and looks at me like that, I feel like the most beautiful woman in the world.

MICHAEL

When Alice stops before me in the room decorated with twinkling lights and filled with the handful of people who are truly important to us, all I can think about is how perfect it all is.

The place.

The time.

The woman.

"Can I go first?" Alice asks. And I dip my chin.

She presses her lips together, and I grip her hands in mine.

"I can't tell you how many times I fantasized about this day. How many times I closed my eyes at night and wished you were by my side. How many moments of my days I spent thinking of you." My chest tightens at her words. "I've loved you for so long, Chef Michael. But even with my birthday wishes, the most I ever wished for was your happiness." She smiles up at me, and my heart grows with each of her words. "All I've ever wanted was for you to be happy." I hold her hands tighter. "I can see it in your eyes, you know? When you look at me, like you are right now, I can see that—by some miracle of the universe—it's me who makes you happy." A single tear trails down Alice's cheek, and it mirrors my own. "You're my real-life fairytale, Mr. Kesso. And this is my real-life happily ever after."

ALICE

"Where are we going?" I can't stop my giggle as Michael hauls me away from our reception and into an elevator.

I may have had too much champagne tonight, especially after those Jell-O shots Suzy snuck into the venue. But is it really possible to have too much at your wedding? Especially when it's New Year's Eve?

Michael smirks down at me as he presses the button for the top floor.

It's the penthouse suite. The biggest, most over-the-top hotel room I've ever laid eyes on.

But I wouldn't care if we were going back to my basement bedroom. The only thing that matters is that it's my wedding night and I'm spending it with Michael.

The elevator doors slide shut, and Michael steps back so he can look at all of me.

"You're fucking beautiful, Mrs. Kesso."

Warmth fills my belly.

"You're not too bad yourself, Mr. Kesso."

It's an understatement. In head-to-toe black, Michael looks the perfect mix of handsome and dangerous.

The doors slide open.

"Come, Wife."

I take Michael's hand and resist making a comment about how I plan to.

We walk in silence to our door, and I wait for Michael to unlock it.

We stayed here last night, in the suite overlooking Minneapolis, so I know what to expect when the door opens.

Except it's not exactly the same.

The lights are all dimmed, and there are overflowing bouquets of flowers in the living room.

I slow, spotting a tray of chocolate-covered berries and a bottle of champagne on the coffee table.

Michael starts to pull me past it, then he pauses.

"Actually..." He reaches down and plucks the bottle out of the bucket of ice. "Now come on, we're almost out of time."

"Out of time?" I quicken my steps to keep up with him.

"You'll see." Michael doesn't turn toward the bedroom. He leads me to the doors to the rooftop terrace.

He drags the door open, and a gust of cold air rolls over us.

I'm about to tell him it's too cold to go outside when I see it.

The dome-shaped tent.

Only it's not a tent exactly, because, as I step out into the night, the city lights bounce off the mirrored walls of the dome.

"We can see out," Michael says as he unzips a hidden door panel. "But no one can see in."

Desire starts to swirl in my center.

I have an idea of what Michael would like to do out here, and I'm ready for it.

When I step inside the little dome, I'm surprised by the warmth—the dim glow of a heater in the corner.

And the rest of the space is filled with... a bed covered in thick blankets and fluffy pillows.

Michael follows me in and secures the door.

"Take your panties off, Mrs. Kesso."

I turn to face him, the bed behind me.

Slowly, I part the sides of my skirt, revealing more and more skin as I go.

Michael shrugs off his suit jacket as he watches.

I reach up under my dress and grip the sides of my panties.

Michael undoes the top two buttons of his shirt.

I tug the lacy material down my legs.

Michael rolls up his sleeves.

I step out of my panties.

Michael holds his hand out for them.

Heat blooms inside me as I place the body-warmed fabric into his hand.

He closes his fist around the material, then shoves them into his pocket. "Sit on the edge of the bed."

I sit.

He removes his belt.

I spread my knees, my skirt splitting to the hip, the material draping between my legs.

He undoes his pants, the zipper loud in the small space.

I reach for the tie at my side.

He pulls the front of his boxer briefs down.

I undo the bow, and the dress loosens, then parts. And my bare breasts spill free.

Michael groans and pulls his dick out.

I stare. My mouth watering.

"Eyes up here." His voice is gravel.

I lift my gaze to meet Michael's as he opens the champagne.

It's dark, but not so dark I can't see his expression.

The hunger in his eyes.

And it's making me tremble.

"Husband, I need you to touch me."

Michael steps between my spread legs, his cock straining toward me.

Strong fingers grip my chin, tipping my head back just a bit more.

"Open your mouth, Wife."

I part my lips. But instead of feeding me his length, Michael brings the champagne bottle up to his mouth.

He swallows, then pours more into his mouth. And dampness pools between my legs.

I get it now.

I open my mouth wider.

He bends over me, and with his eyes on mine, he parts his lips, and the champagne falls from his mouth into mine.

And the sky erupts above us.

Fireworks fill the night.

The taste. The explosions. All of it lights my body on fire.

Michael applies pressure on my chin. "Swallow."

I close my mouth and swallow.

Michael lowers to his knees before me.

The low bed is the perfect height. And his body lines up with mine.

Michael holds the bottle up to my mouth as he presses the tip of his dick against my wet entrance.

I tip my head back again, and this time he pours the liquid directly into my mouth.

I keep it there.

The bubbles dancing on my tongue.

Michael sets the bottle down, then grabs my hip with one hand and the back of my head with the other.

Michael tilts his mouth below mine.

I press my lips to his parted ones, and as I push the champagne out of my mouth and into his, he shoves his hips forward.

He fills me as he takes from me.

He fucks me as he makes love to me.

And under the exploding sky, we melt into each other.

Becoming one.

EPILOGUE TWO – MICHAEL

"Hurry!" Alice calls from the study.

"I'm right here, Baby." I step through the doorway, two glasses of wine in hand.

Alice looks up from her spot on the couch, snuggled under her favorite blanket with a laptop balanced on her lap. "Oh, good idea." She takes the glass I hold out for her.

Careful not to spill, I slide into the spot next to Alice and prop my feet on the coffee table.

It's been three months since Alice became my wife, and every day is better than the last.

Even with filming only now starting up again for *Second Bite*, we've been busy since the New Year started—traveling, getting the foundation ready.

So, as a way to celebrate the launch of the Chef Mike and Alice Cooking Classes, we decided to rent a place in the mountains.

Alice suggested going back to the cabin in Bear Cove, but we both agreed we could find something with the same feel that doesn't also have the creeper memories.

Though, to be fair, since Mr. Forde has recovered the backlist of photos, we have looked through them. Many times. Without clothes on. So it's not all bad.

I drape my arm over the back of the couch behind Alice.

This is just a rental house, but I think I'll put an offer on it. Our lives are only going to get busier after tonight, and having a little forest retreat might be just the thing.

"One minute." Alice chews her lip.

I squeeze her shoulder. "Did they confirm that our end of the site would update in real time?"

We did what we discussed, selecting eight cities across the country to host classes, and now it's just a matter of filling the spots.

Alice nods but still hits the refresh button on the website. "Yeah. The sale will open on the hour, first come, first served." She blows out a breath. "What if no one signs up? It's so expensive."

"People will sign up, Baby Cakes. We might not sell out in the first five minutes like a Zelle concert, but we'll fill every seat, I promise."

"I really hope so," Alice says.

A second later, the clock in the corner of her screen clicks over.

"It's live," she whispers.

We stare at the screen, the crackling fireplace across the room the only thing breaking the silence.

I open my mouth to remind her I'm proud of her. To tell her that no matter how long it takes, I love her so much.

But before I can say anything, the column for Minneapolis lights up.

A moment later, the first name appears, claiming two tickets.
Mr. and Mrs. Eklund.
Alice squeaks. "We sold a pair!"
Another set populates.
Mr. and Mrs. Vass.
Alice gasps.

Then another couple.

Mr. and Mrs. Gonzalez.

Alice lifts a hand to her mouth.

Another two tickets are sold. A singular name on both.

Nero.

I turn to Alice, lifting my glass to tap against hers. "Looks like our first class will be in Minnesota."

ABOUT THE AUTHOR

S. J. Tilly was born and raised in the glorious state of Minnesota but now resides in the mountains of Colorado. To avoid the snowy winters, S. J. enjoys burying her head in books, whether to read them or write them or listen to them.

When she's not busy writing her contemporary smut, she can be found lounging with Mr. Tilly and their circus of rescue boxers.

To stay up to date on all things Tilly, make sure to follow her on her socials, join her newsletter, and interact whenever you feel like it! Links to everything on her website www.sjtilly.com

LOVE LETTERS SERIES

Contemporary Romance
Love, Utley
Hannah

Maddox Lovelace. The captivating football player I met in college.

The one I only knew for a week. A week that was... life-changing.

Until my phone rang, and I had no choice but to go home.

I left Maddox a letter, putting my feelings on paper, giving him my number, hoping he'd call.

But he didn't call.

He never called.

He got drafted into the professional league and lived like a king while I stayed home and struggled to stay afloat.

I may have followed his career, but now that he's retired from football, I've forced myself to stop thinking about him.

And it's okay that I won't ever see him again. That week in college was fifteen years ago.

I'm not in love with Maddox anymore.

I might even hate him.

Maddox

Hannah Utley. The name that's haunted me since my senior year of college.

The girl who caught my attention with her wide eyes and freckled nose.

Who spent one week twisting up my insides until she stole a piece of my heart the night we got locked inside the campus library.

The girl who disappeared without a word.

It's the name of the girl I've been trying to forget for fifteen years.

And it's the name looking up at me from the résumé in my hand.

Because Hannah Utley works for the company I just purchased.

And that makes her mine. Whether she likes it or not.

Tackled in the Stacks

I caught her staring at me from across the quad, eyes fixed on the football jersey stretched across my wide chest. And if I flexed my muscles, showing off the strength of a defensive tackle, it was just to see her blush.

And then she did, and I couldn't get her out of my mind.

Her wide eyes. The freckles on her cheeks.

I needed to know her. The girl who scampered away every time we bumped into each other—by accident and by design. The girl who shyly agreed to come to my game, getting her first taste of football. The girl, Hannah Utley, who worked at the campus library and let me rest my head on her shoulder as she read to me in one of the study rooms.

It was innocent. Mostly.

Until we lose track of time and discover that the library has closed. And we're locked inside.

Now it's me and Hannah in the stacks.

Alone.

With nothing but desire between us.

Alliance Series

Dark Mafia Romance

NERO

Payton

Running away from home at seventeen wasn't easy. Let's face it, though, nothing before, or in the ten years since, has ever been easy for me.

And I'm doing okay. Sorta. I just need to keep scraping by, living under the radar. Staying out of people's way, off people's minds.

So when a man walks through my open patio door, stepping boldly into my home and my life, I should be scared. Frightened. Terrified.

But I must be more broken than I realized because I'm none of those things.

I'm intrigued.

And I'm wondering if the way to take control of my life is by giving in to him.

Nero

The first time I took a man's life, I knew there'd be no going back. No normal existence in the cards for me.

So instead of walking away, I climbed a mountain of bodies and created my own destiny. By forming The Alliance.

And I was fine with that. Content enough to carry on.

Until I stepped through those open doors and into her life.

I should've walked away. Should've gone right back out the door I came through. But I didn't.

And now her life is in danger.

But that's the thing about being a bad man. I'll happily paint the streets red to protect what's mine.

And Payton is mine. Whether she knows it or not.

KING

Okay, so, my bad for assuming the guy I was going on a date with *wasn't* married. And my bad for taking him to a friend's house for dinner, only to find out my friend is also friends with *his* wife. Because, in fact, he *is* married. And she happens to be at my friend's house because her husband was *busy working*.

Confused? So am I.

Unsurprisingly, my date's wife is super angry about finding out that her husband is a cheating asshole.

Girl, I get it.

Then, to make matters more convoluted, there is the man sitting next to my date's wife. A man named King, who is apparently her brother and who lives up to his name.

And since my *date* is a two-timing prick, I'm not going to feel bad about drooling over King,

especially since I'll never see him again.

Or at least I don't plan to.

I plan to take an Uber to the cheater's apartment to get my car keys.

I plan for it to be quick.

And if I had to list a thousand possible outcomes... witnessing my date's murder, being kidnapped by his killer, and then being forced to marry the super attractive but clearly

deranged crime lord would not have been on my Bingo card.

But alas, here I am.

DOM

VAL

When I was nine, I went to my first funeral. Along with accepting my father's death, I had to accept new and awful truths I wasn't prepared for.

When I was nineteen, I went to my mother's funeral. We weren't close, but with her gone, I became more alone than ever before.

Sure, I have a half brother who runs The Alliance. And yeah, he's given me his protection—in the form of a bodyguard and chauffeur. But I don't have anyone that really knows me. No one to really love me.

Until I meet him. The man in the airport.

And when one chance meeting turns into something hotter, something more serious, I let myself believe that maybe he's the one. Maybe this man is the one who will finally save me from my loneliness. The one to give me the family I've always craved.

DOM

The Mafia is in my blood. It's what I do.

So when that blood is spilled and one funeral turns into three, drastic measures need to be taken.

And when this battle turns into a war, I'm going to need more men. More power.

I'm going to need The Alliance.

And I'll become a member. By any means necessary.

HANS

Vengeance is rarely clean.

Sin Series

Romantic Suspense

Mr. Sin

I should have run the other way. Paid my tab and gone back to my room. But he was there. And he was… everything. I figured, what's the harm in letting passion rule my decisions for one night? So what if he looks like the Devil in a suit? I'd be leaving in the morning. Flying home, back to my pleasant but predictable life. I'd never see him again.

Except I do. In the last place I expected. And now everything I've worked so hard for is in jeopardy.

We can't stop what we've started, but this is bigger than the two of us.

And when his past comes back to haunt him, love might not be enough to save me.

Sin Too

Beth

It started with tragedy.

And secrets.

Hidden truths that refused to stay buried have come out to chase me. Now I'm on the run, living under a blanket of constant fear, pretending to be someone I'm not. And if I'm not really me, how am I supposed to know what's real?

Angelo

Watch the girl.

It was supposed to be a simple assignment. But like everything else in this family, there's nothing simple about it. Not my task. Not her fake name. And not my feelings for her.

But Beth is mine now.

So when the monsters from her past come out to play, they'll have to get through me first.

Miss Sin

I'm so sick of watching the world spin by. Of letting people think I'm plain and boring, too afraid to just be myself.

Then I see *him*.

John.

He's strength and fury and unapologetic.

He's everything I want. And everything I wish I was.

He won't want me, but that doesn't matter. The sight of him is all the inspiration I need to finally shatter this glass house I've built around myself.

Only he does want me. And when our worlds collide, details we can't see become tangled, twisting together, ensnaring us in an invisible trap.

When it all goes wrong, I don't know if I'll be able to break free of the chains binding us or if I'll suffocate in the process.

Sleet Series

Hockey Romantic Comedy

Sleet Kitten

There are a few things that life doesn't prepare you for. Like what to do when a super-hot guy catches you sneaking around in his basement. Or what to do when a mysterious package shows up with tickets to a hockey game, because apparently, he's a professional athlete. Or how to handle it when you get to the game and realize he's freaking famous since half of the 20,000 people in the stands are wearing his jersey.

I thought I was a well-adjusted adult, reasonably prepared for life. But one date with Jackson Wilder, a viral video, and a "I didn't know she was your mom" incident, and I'm suddenly questioning everything I thought I knew.

But he's fun. And great. And I think I might be falling for him. But I don't know if he's falling for me too, or if he's as much of a player off the ice as on.

Sleet Sugar

My friends have convinced me. No more hockey players.

With a dad who is the head coach for the Minnesota Sleet, it seemed like an easy decision.

My friends have also convinced me that the best way to boost my fragile self-esteem is through a one-night stand.

A dating app. A hotel bar. A sexy-as-hell man, who's sweet and funny, and did I mention, sexy as hell... I fortified my courage and invited myself up to his room.

Assumptions. There's a rule about them.

I assumed he was passing through town. I assumed he was a businessman or maybe an investor or accountant or literally anything other than a professional hockey player. I assumed I'd never see him again.

I assumed wrong.

Sleet Banshee

Mother-freaking hockey players. My friends found their happily ever afters with a couple of sweet, doting, over-the-top, in-love athletes. They got nicknames like *Kitten* and *Sugar*. But me? I got stuck with a dickhead who riles me up on purpose and calls me *Banshee*. Yeah, he might have a voice made specifically for wet dreams. And he might have a body and face carved by the gods. And he might have a level of Alpha-hole that gets me all hot and bothered.

But when he presses my buttons, he presses ALL of my buttons. And I'm not the type of girl who takes things sitting down. And I only got caught on my knees that one time. In the museum.

But when one of my decisions gets one of my friends hurt... I can't stop blaming myself. And him.

Except he can't take a hint. And I can't keep my panties on.

Darling Series

Contemporary Small Town Romance
Smoky Darling

Elouise

I fell in love with Beckett when I was seven.

He broke my heart when I was fifteen.

When I was eighteen, I promised myself I'd forget about him.

And I did. For a dozen years.

But now he's back home. Here. In Darling Lake. And I don't know if I should give in to the temptation swirling between us or run the other way.

Beckett

She had a crush on me when she was a kid. But she was my brother's best friend's little sister. I didn't see her like that. And even if I had, she was too young. Our age difference was too great.

But now I'm back home. And she's here. And she's all the way grown up.

It wouldn't have worked back then. But I'll be damned if I won't get a taste of her now.

Latte Darling

I have a nice life—living in my hometown, owning the coffee shop I've worked at since I was sixteen.

It's comfortable.

On paper.

But I'm tired of doing everything by myself. Tired of being in charge of every decision in my life.

I want someone to lean on. Someone to spend time with. Sit with. Hug.

And I really don't want to go to my best friend's wedding alone.

So, I signed up for a dating app and agreed to meet with the first guy who messaged me.

And now here I am, at the bar.

Only it's not my date that just sat down in the chair across from me. It's his dad.

And holy hell, he's the definition of silver fox. If a silver fox can be thick as a house, have piercing blue eyes and tattoos from his neck down to his fingertips.

He's giving me *big bad wolf* vibes. Only instead of running, I'm blushing. And he looks like he might just want to eat me whole.

Tilly World Holiday Novellas

Second Bite

When a holiday baking competition goes incredibly wrong. Or right...

Michael

I'm starting to think I've been doing this for too long. The screaming fans. The constant media attention. The fat paychecks. None of it brings me the happiness I yearn for.

Yet here I am. Another year. Another holiday special. Another Christmas spent alone in a hotel room.

But then the lights go up. And I see *her*.

Alice

It's an honor to be a contestant, I know that. But right now, it feels a little like punishment. Because any second, Chef Michael Kesso, the man I've been in love with for years, the man who doesn't even know I exist, is going to walk onto the set, and it will be a miracle if I don't pass out at the sight of him.

But the time for doubts is over. Because *Second Bite* is about to start "in three... two... one..."

www.ingramcontent.com/pod-product-compliance
Lightning Source LLC
Chambersburg PA
CBHW051309170626
46809CB00004B/1820